KING MIDAS

AND THE GOLDEN TOUCH

By Al Perkins

Illustrated by Harold Berson

BEGINNER BOOKS   A Division of Random House, Inc.

This title was originally catalogued by the Library of Congress as follows: Perkins, Al. King Midas and the golden touch. Illustrated by Harold Berson. [New York] Beginner Books [ᶜ1969] 62 p. col. illus. 24 cm.   King Midas enjoyed turning everything he touched to gold until he discovered that gold food was hard to eat and gold daughters cold to hug. [1. Midas. 2. Mythology, Greek] I. Berson, Harold, illus. II. Title. PZ8.1.P4Ki 398.2 70—85290 ISBN 0-394-80054-0 ISBN 0-394-90054-5 (lib. bdg.)

I J K L   2 3 4

KING MIDAS

AND THE GOLDEN TOUCH

King Midas loved gold.

He slept in a golden bed.

He kept a bluebird in a golden cage.

Every morning the bluebird
sang to wake him up.

3

Every morning the King put on
his golden crown.
He sat down to breakfast
with his daughter, Princess Leela.

4

They drank royal grape juice.

They ate royal sausages.

They drank from golden cups.

They ate from golden plates.

After breakfast the King went
to see his royal goldsmiths.
His goldsmiths made him
golden clocks, and golden tables.

They even made him golden fish hooks.

Every day the King went for a ride.
He went all over his land
looking for gold.
Then he took the gold
back to his palace.

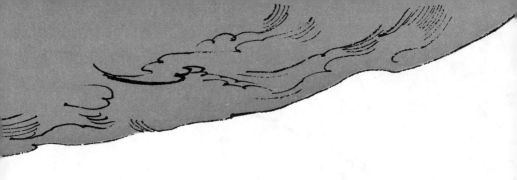

In the palace, his servants
took the gold downstairs.
The King unlocked a secret door.

The servants took the gold
into a big, dark cave.
The cave was full of gold.

Every day King Midas
locked himself in.

"Gold!" he would say.
"I love the way it shines."

"Gold!" he would say.

"I love the way it feels."

"Gold! Gold! Gold!
How I love my gold!"

One day the King was in his cave.

He heard a sound. He looked up.

He saw a strange little man.

"How did you get in here?" he asked.

"Oh, I can do anything,"
said the little man.
"Why, I can even
make a wish come true.
What do you wish for most?"

"What do I wish for most?
Gold, of course!" said the King.
"I wish that everything I touch
would turn to gold."

"That is a very big wish,"
said the little man.
"It may not make you happy.
But if that is what you want . . ."

". . . I will make your wish come true.
Go upstairs. Go to bed.
In the morning everything you touch
will turn to gold."

There was a flash of light.
The little man was gone.

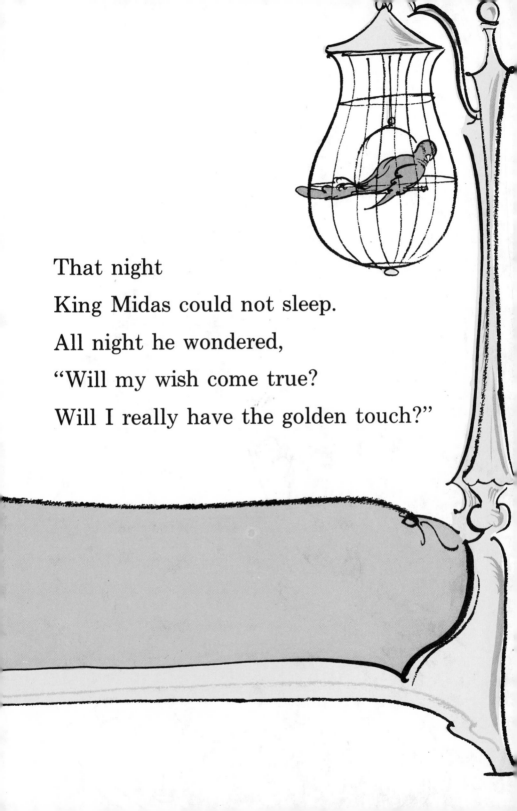

That night
King Midas could not sleep.
All night he wondered,
"Will my wish come true?
Will I really have the golden touch?"

At last the sun came up.

The King's bluebird began to sing.
King Midas sat up.
He reached out to touch the bird.

The bluebird turned to gold.

"It works!" shouted King Midas.

"I have the golden touch!"

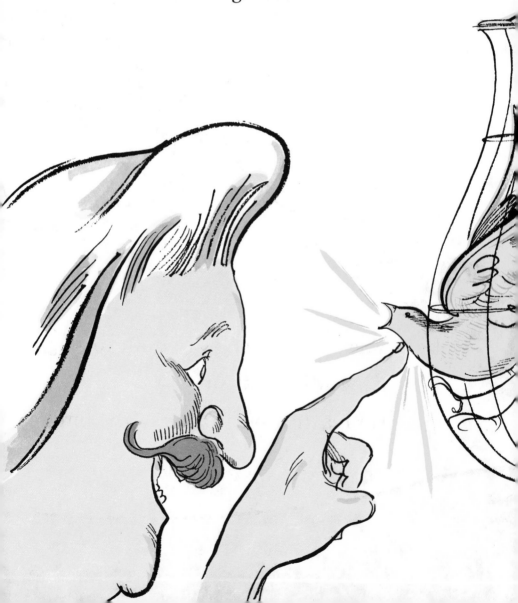

He put on his royal coat and pants.

His coat and pants turned to gold!

King Midas ran through his palace.

He turned a door to gold.

He turned a chair to gold.

He turned his umbrella to gold.

Then he ran into the garden.
He turned a frog to gold.

He touched the red roses.
He turned them all to gold.
"Look!" he called to Princess Leela.
"Look what I can do!"

But Leela did not answer.

She just looked at the golden roses.

They were hard and cold.

They did not even smell.

The King and the Princess
went to eat breakfast.
King Midas was very happy.
He took a royal sausage.

"Ouch!" yelled King Midas.

"My sausage has turned to gold!"

"I can't eat this!" he cried.

He reached for his grape juice.

"Oh my!" said King Midas.

"Golden grape juice!"

"I must have food!
I'm hungry!" he shouted.

He ran into the royal kitchen.
He grabbed a fish.
It turned to gold.

He grabbed apples and doughnuts.

He grabbed more and more sausages.

The same thing happened.

The same thing happened all day long.

The King couldn't write.

His ink turned to gold.

He couldn't make a fire.

The logs turned to gold.

All the King's servants ran away.
No one could work
in a palace like this.

That night the King
tried to brush his teeth.

He tried to take a bath.

He tried to go to bed.

But there was nothing he could do.

King Midas sat on his golden bed.

He began to cry.

Princess Leela heard her father.
She came into his room.

"Poor Daddy," said Leela.
"Please don't cry."

She ran to her father.
She held out her arms.

King Midas reached out.
He touched his little girl.

Leela turned into
a statue of gold.

Day after day King Midas sat
on his golden throne
in his golden palace.
He looked and he looked
at his cold, gold daughter.

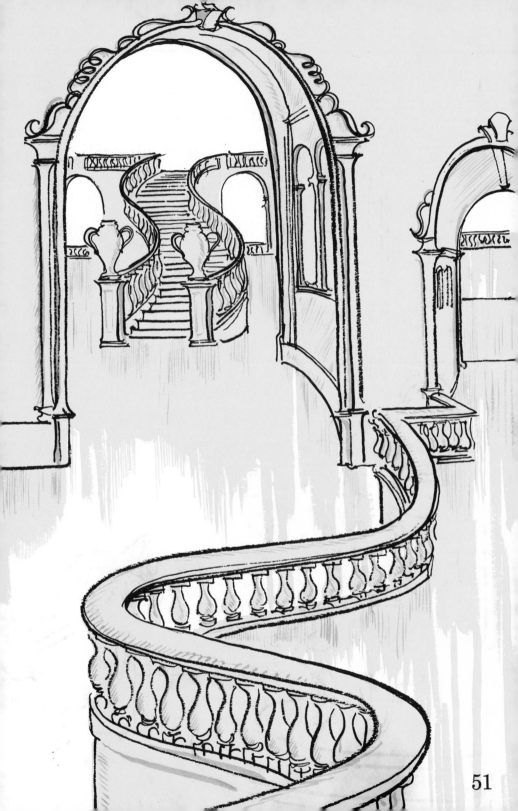

51

Then one day,
there was a flash of light.
King Midas looked up.
The little man was back!

"King Midas," said the little man,
"I think I will give you
one more wish.
If you love something
more than gold,
wish for it, King Midas.
Wish for it with all your heart!"

King Midas jumped up.

And he wished with all his heart.

He put out his hand.

He touched his cold, gold daughter.

His wish came true.

He had turned his daughter
back from gold!
They ran through the palace.
The King touched everything.
He turned everything back
into what it was before.

He touched the roses.

He touched the frog.

He touched the umbrella.

He touched the bluebird.

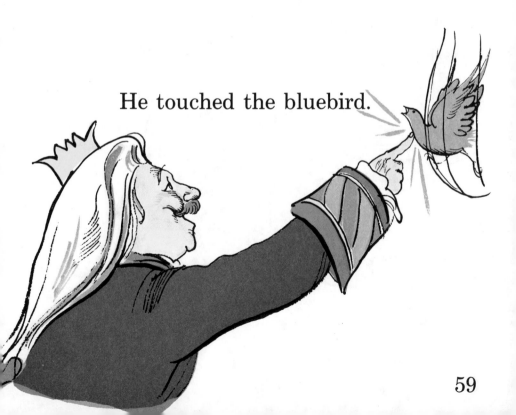

59

Last of all,

he touched the royal sausages

and the royal grape juice.

Then King Midas and Princess Leela
sat down to breakfast.
It was the happiest breakfast
they had ever had.